MARY HOFFMAN studied English at Cambridge, and linguistics
at University College, London. A well-known writer and journalist,
she has actively campaigned against sexism and racism in children's
literature for more than 20 years. She is the author of over forty books
for children, including *Amazing Grace*, its sequel *Grace and Family*,
and *An Angel Just Like Me*, all for Frances Lincoln. Mary lives
in London, with her husband and their three daughters.

CAROLINE BINCH studied graphic design at Salford Technical College.
She has been described by 'The Guardian' as "a superb artist,
specialising in portraying a vivaciously heightened reality
that we can all recognise." In 1993 her illustrations for *Hue Boy*,
written by Rita Phillips Mitchell, won the Smarties Prize. As well
as illustrating the *Grace* books, Caroline has written and illustrated
Gregory Cool and *Since Dad Left*, both published by Frances Lincoln.
She lives near Penzance in Cornwall.

For Buchi Emecheta   *M.H.*
For Joe *C.B.*

Amazing Grace copyright © Frances Lincoln Limited 1991
Text copyright © Mary Hoffman 1991
Illustrations copyright © Caroline Binch 1991

First published in Great Britain in 1991 by
Frances Lincoln Limited, 4 Torriano Mews
Torriano Avenue, London NW5 2RZ

British Library Cataloguing in Publication Data
available on request

ISBN 0-7112-0670-8 hardback
ISBN 0-7112-0699-6 paperback

Set in Garamond

Printed in Hong Kong

20 22 24 23 21 19

Amazing Grace

Mary Hoffman

Illustrated by
Caroline Binch

FRANCES LINCOLN

Grace was a girl who loved stories.

She didn't mind if they were read to her or told to her or made up in her own head. She didn't care if they were from books or on TV or in films or on the video or out of Nana's long memory. Grace just loved stories.

And after she had heard them, or sometimes while they were still going on, Grace would act them out. And she always gave herself the most exciting part.

Grace went into battle as Joan of Arc . . .

and wove a wicked web as Anansi the spiderman.

She hid inside the wooden horse at the gates of Troy . . .

she crossed the Alps with Hannibal and a hundred elephants . . .

she sailed the seven seas
with a peg-leg
and a parrot.

She was Hiawatha, sitting by the shining Big-Sea-Water

and Mowgli in the back garden jungle.

But most of all Grace loved to act pantomimes. She liked to be Dick Whittington turning to hear the bells of London Town or Aladdin rubbing the magic lamp. The best characters in pantomimes were boys, but Grace played them anyway.

When there was no-one else around, Grace played
all the parts herself. She was a cast of thousands.
Paw-Paw the cat usually helped out.

And sometimes she could persuade Ma and Nana
to join in, when they weren't too busy. Then she
was Doctor Grace and their lives were in her hands.

One day at school her teacher said they were going to do the play of *Peter Pan*. Grace put up her hand to be . . . Peter Pan.

"You can't be called Peter," said Raj. "That's a boy's name."

But Grace kept her hand up.

"You can't be Peter Pan," whispered Natalie. "He wasn't black." But Grace kept her hand up.

"All right," said the teacher. "Lots of you want to be Peter Pan, so we'll have to have auditions. We'll choose the parts next Monday."

When Grace got home, she
seemed rather sad.
"What's the matter?"
asked Ma.
"Raj said I couldn't be
Peter Pan because I'm a girl."
"That just shows all Raj
knows about it," said Ma.
"Peter Pan is *always* a girl!"

Grace cheered up, then later she remembered
something else. "Natalie says I can't be Peter Pan
because I'm black," she said.

Ma started to get angry but Nana stopped her.

"It seems that Natalie is another one who don't
know nothing," she said. "You can be anything
you want, Grace, if you put your mind to it."

ROSALIE
WILKINS
in
ROMEO & JULIET

ROMEO AND JULIET

ROSALIE WILKINS

STUNNING NEW

Next day was Saturday and Nana told
Grace they were going out. In the
afternoon they caught a bus and a
train into town. Nana took Grace to a
grand theatre. Outside it said,
"ROSALIE WILKINS in ROMEO AND JULIET"
in beautiful sparkling lights.

"Are we going to the ballet, Nana?" asked Grace.

"We are, Honey, but I want you to look at these pictures first."

Nana showed Grace some photographs of a beautiful young girl dancer in a tutu. "STUNNING NEW JULIET!" it said on one of them.

"That one is little Rosalie from back home in Trinidad," said Nana. "Her Granny and me, we grew up together on the island. She's always asking me do I want tickets to see her little girl dance – so this time I said yes."

After the ballet, Grace played the part of Juliet,
dancing around her room in her imaginary tutu.
"I can be anything I want," she thought. "I can
even be Peter Pan."

On Monday they had the auditions. Their teacher let the class vote on the parts. Raj was chosen to play Captain Hook. Natalie was going to be Wendy.

Then they had to choose Peter Pan.

Grace knew exactly what to do – and all the words to say. It was a part she had often played at home. All the children voted for her.

"You were great," said Natalie.

The play was a great success and Grace was an
amazing Peter Pan.

After it was all over, she said, "I feel as if I could
fly all the way home!"

"You probably could," said Ma.

"Yes," said Nana. "If Grace put her mind to it –
she can do anything she want."

MORE PICTURE BOOKS IN PAPERBACK
FROM FRANCES LINCOLN

GREGORY COOL

Caroline Binch

When a cool city boy meets the full warmth of the Caribbean,
anything can happen... Gregory is determined not to enjoy himself
when he is sent off to visit his grandparents in rural Tobago. After a whole
variety of adventures, however, he begins to think that life outside the city
may not be so bad after all.

Suitable for National Curriculum English - Reading, Key Stages 1 and 2
Scottish Guidelines English Language - Reading, Level C

ISBN 0-7112-0890-5   £4.99

CHINYE

Obi Onyefulu

Illustrated by Evie Safarewicz

Poor Chinye! Back and forth through the forest she goes, fetching and carrying
for her cruel stepmother. But strange powers are watching over her, and soon
her life will be magically transformed... An enchanting retelling of a traditional
West African folk-tale of goodness, greed and a treasure-house of gold.

Suitable for National Curriculum English - Reading, Key Stages 1 and 2
Scottish Guidelines, English Language - Reading, Levels B and C

ISBN 0-7112-1052-7   £4.99

THE FIRE CHILDREN

Eric Maddern

Illustrated by Frané Lessac

Why are some people black, some white, and others yellow, pink or brown?
This intriguing West African creation myth tells how the first spirit-people
solve their loneliness using clay and fire – and fill the Earth with children
of every colour under the sun!

Selected for Children's Books of the Year 1993

Suitable for National Curriculum English - Reading, Key Stages 1 and 2
Scottish Guidelines English Language - Reading, Levels B and C ; Environmental Studies, Level C

ISBN 0-7112-0885-9   £4.99

Frances Lincoln titles are available from all good bookshops.

Prices are correct at time of publication, but may be subject to change.